Bears at the Beach

Emma Carlisle

Macmillan Children's Books

Today we went on an adventure.

Dad packed a parasol, Mum rolled a giant towel, and I brought my brand new kite.

I couldn't wait to fly it!

Bears at
the Beach

for my
mum and dad

First published 2016 by Macmillan Children's Books,

an imprint of Pan Macmillan,

20 New Wharf Road, London N1 9RR.

Associated companies throughout the world.

www.panmacmillan.com

ISBN: 978-1-4472-5744-8 (HB)

ISBN: 978-1-4472-5745-5 (PB)

Text and illustrations © Emma Carlisle 2016

Moral rights asserted. All rights reserved.

A CIP catalogue record for this book is

available from the British Library.

2 4 6 8 9 7 5 3 1

Printed in China

And even though I was excited,

I sat still and didn't wriggle,

as me, Mum and Dad all went to...

"I'm going to lie down and read," said Mum.

But the beach is not for lying on, it's for playing on!

So that's what we did.

Then we went on a boat around the bay.

After lunch I couldn't wait to fly my kite.

But Mum and Dad said there was no wind and I needed the wind to help me.

But my kite wanted to fly, I could tell! So I ran and ran as fast as I could.

"Mum, Dad, look!"

But when I turned around,
I couldn't see Mum and Dad
anywhere. I was lost!

They weren't by
the ice creams,

or by the
sandcastles,

and they weren't
having a swim.

I searched up high,

and I searched
down low.

I even searched round and round!

It was starting to feel cold
and I was getting hungry.
Some families started to
go home...

I wished I could
go home too.

Then suddenly,
I wasn't just lost...

But nobody on the beach could hear me, it was far too windy. "Go away wind!" I said.

But then I had
an idea!

It was a
very good idea.

"There he is!"
cried Mum and Dad.

"We've been looking
everywhere for you!"

"It looks like it was windy enough to fly your kite," said Dad.

"And we're very lucky it was," said Mum.

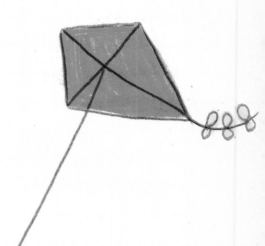

They said I was a very clever bear.

Dad packed up the parasol, Mum rolled up the giant towel,

and I told them all about my adventure.

Mum and Dad said I wasn't to run off again, and I promised I wouldn't.

I said "Being at the beach is only fun when you are both here with me."

Peep! Peep! "All aboard!"

It was getting very
late, so we all had
to run...

...and jump on the train!

I sat still and didn't wriggle,

as me, Mum and Dad went all the way...

home.

Blue Kangaroo belonged to Lily.
He was her very own kangaroo.
Sometimes, Lily would say, "Do you
remember when I first met you?"
And Blue Kangaroo would smile while
Lily told him the whole story all over again.

It seemed like ages and ages ago. Lily had been waiting for the day when her new baby brother, Jack, would come home for the first time.

When I First Met You, Blue Kangaroo!

Emma Chichester Clark

HarperCollins *Children's Books*

In memory of Margot Martini, the little girl who sparked a movement.

Collect all the fantastic books about Blue Kangaroo!

Where Are You, Blue Kangaroo?

It Was You, Blue Kangaroo!

What Shall We Do, Blue Kangaroo?

I'll Show You, Blue Kangaroo!

Merry Christmas, Blue Kangaroo!

Happy Birthday, Blue Kangaroo!

Come to School Too, Blue Kangaroo!

First published in hardback in Great Britain by HarperCollins Children's Books in 2015

1 3 5 7 9 10 8 6 4 2

HarperCollins Children's Books is a division of HarperCollins Publishers Ltd.

ISBN: 978-0-00-742510-5

Text and illustrations copyright © Emma Chichester Clark 2015

Visit our website at: www.harpercollins.co.uk

Printed in China

"They're here! They're here!" she cried.
She was so looking forward to helping with everything!

She began straight away!
"Here you are, Mum," she said as she took her
some juice and cookies.
"Thank you, Lily," said her mother. "Be careful
with that tray!"

"Oh! Lily! Look out!"
But it was too late! The vase tipped over…
water and flowers splashed all over Jack's cradle.
"Oh, Lily!" sighed her mother.

Jack screamed and screamed.
"It's all right, Lily," said her mother. "It was an accident."
"Sorry, Jack," said Lily.

When Lily's dad was looking after Jack, Lily said,
"He really can't do anything by himself, can he?"
"That's why he needs you, Lily," said her father.
"Why don't you read to him?"

Lily showed Jack the pictures in her book.
"Here's a cow," she said. "It goes 'mooo!'
And here's a sheep. It goes 'baaa!'
And here's a tiger…" she said,

"…it goes 'RRRRRROOOOOAAAARRRR!'"
Jack shrieked! He screamed and screamed!
"Oh, Lily!" said her father. "That's much too loud!"
"Sorry, Jack," said Lily.

One day, Jack was in his pram in the garden.
"Hello, Jack!" said Lily.

"Shall I rock you and sing a lullaby?
Rock-a-bye baby on the tree top…" she sang.

"When the wind blows, the cradle will rock…"
Lily's singing grew louder and louder.
The pram bounced up and down…
Jack began to cry.

Then he
screamed
and screamed.

"Oh, Lily!"
cried her mother.
"That's much too rough!"
"Sorry, Jack," said Lily.

"I don't think Jack loves me, because he cries whenever I go near him," said Lily.
"Of course he loves you!" said her father. "You just need to be gentle with him."

The next day, Lily's grandma came.
"I've got a surprise for you, Lily!" she said.
"I've brought someone who needs looking after!"

Lily's surprise had soft blue ears,
little black eyes, whiskers and a
long blue tail. It was a blue kangaroo!
"Oh!" cried Lily. "I LOVE him!"

Everyone said hello to
Blue Kangaroo.
"I'm going to look after him
for ever and ever!" said Lily.

And Blue Kangaroo
knew he'd come
to the right person.

At bedtime, after Jack's bath, Lily said it was time to bath Blue Kangaroo.
"You'll love it!" she said, as she gently put him in the water.

But Blue Kangaroo wasn't so sure.

"Oh, Blue Kangaroo!" said Lily. "I do love looking after you!"
She sprinkled him with Jack's talcum powder... but it
came out faster than she expected.

It stuck to the wet kangaroo
like glue!
"OH, NO!" cried Lily.
"What's happened to you?"

"Oh dear!
Oh dear!"
thought poor
Blue Kangaroo.

"MUM!" cried Lily.
"Look what I've done!"
"Oh, Lily!" said her mother.

"He'll be all right," said Lily's mother as she gently washed Blue Kangaroo.
"I'm just no good at looking after babies!" said Lily.
"He won't love me now."
"It was just a mistake," said Lily's mother.

"We all make mistakes," she said
as she put Blue Kangaroo in the
airing cupboard to dry.
"You don't!" said Lily.
"That's because I practised on
you!" said Lily's mother.

"Oh…" thought
Blue Kangaroo. "So
Lily needs to practise too."

"Did you make mistakes with me?" asked Lily.
"I make mistakes all the time!" said her mother.
"And I still love you!" said Lily.
"And I love you!" said her mother. "And so do Jack and Blue Kangaroo!"

Lily lay in the dark thinking about her new baby brother and her new Blue Kangaroo. Everything was new. She had never looked after anyone smaller than she was. There were so many new things to learn.

Meanwhile, Blue Kangaroo was feeling better, but he was missing Lily.
"I'd better go and give her a chance to practise looking after me!" he thought.

He jumped a beautiful kangaroo jump,

and landed softly on the floor.

Then he tiptoed
along the passage
to Lily's room.

"Blue Kangaroo!" whispered Lily. "How did you get here?
I didn't know you could do that!"

Blue Kangaroo hopped across the floor and up on to the bed, into Lily's arms.

"Oh, Blue Kangaroo, how clever of you! Will you
help me look after baby Jack too?" said Lily.
She hugged him tight and Blue Kangaroo smiled
his secret smile.
"I knew I'd love you," said Lily, "when I first met you!"
"And I knew I'd love you!" thought Blue Kangaroo.